The BERENSTAIN BEARS

Answers begin on p. 61.

A GOLDEN BOOK®
Western Publishing Company, Inc.
Racine, Wisconsin 53404
No part of this book may be reproduced or copied in any form
® without written permission from the publisher. Produced in U.S.A.

Find the Difference

These two pictures seem to look exactly alike, but look again!

Can you find 5 things in the top picture that
are missing from the bottom picture?

2

Beary Tales

When Mama reads aloud, the stories seem to come alive!
Can you find 5 fairy-tale characters hiding in Brother and Sister's room?

Hive Hunt

One of Grizzly Gramps' bees is lost!
Help him find the way to the hive.

GRIZZLY GRAMPS'
HONEY STAND

Alphabet Mess

Brother and Sister are playing an alphabet game while they clean up their room.

Brother picks up all the things that start with the letter **A**.
Can you circle each one?

Sister picks up all the things that start with the letter **B**.
Can you put an X through each one?

All Dressed Up!

Mama wants to buy a new dress just like her old favorite.
Help her by drawing a circle around the dress that looks
exactly like the one she is wearing.

Haze Maze

It's such a foggy day, Sister can't find
her way! Can *you* show her the way home?

Squirrel Search

There are 10 squirrels hiding in the treehouse. Can you find them all?

Firefly Fun

Brother and Sister are catching fireflies.
How many fireflies are in the jar?
How many are still free?
How many fireflies are there all together?

$$\begin{array}{r} 4 \\ +\ 5 \\ \hline 9 \end{array}$$

Big and Little Raindrops

Brother and Sister like to watch the raindrops.
Help them find the 3 biggest raindrops. Circle them.
Now circle the 3 littlest raindrops.

Lots of Stars

Sister and Brother are looking
at the stars. How many do they see?

A Frog Is a Frog Is a Frog

Brother Bear is happy. The opposite of **happy** is **sad.** Trace the line from the happy frog to the sad frog. Now match up the other opposites by drawing a line from one to the other.

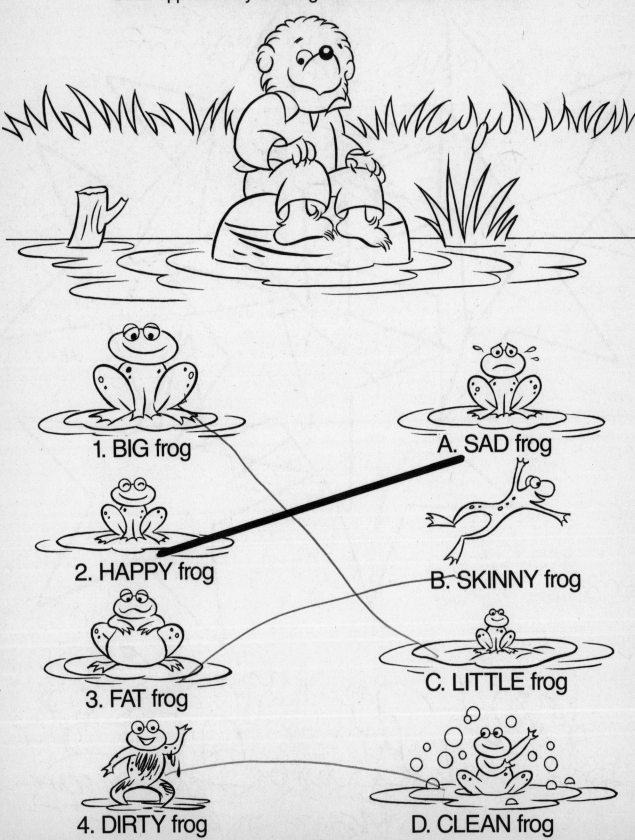

1. BIG frog

2. HAPPY frog

3. FAT frog

4. DIRTY frog

A. SAD frog

B. SKINNY frog

C. LITTLE frog

D. CLEAN frog

In the Mood for Food

Mama and the cubs want to feed the birds, but they can't find them. Can you find 9 birds hiding in the tree?

Christmas Cookies

Can you help Mama finish baking her Christmas cookies? Draw in the missing cookie in each row.

Cane Game

There are 4 candy canes hanging on
the tree. Can you find them all?

Letter Getter

Raffish Ralph ran off with the first letters of these rhyming words.
Look at the picture clues. Then fill in the missing letters.

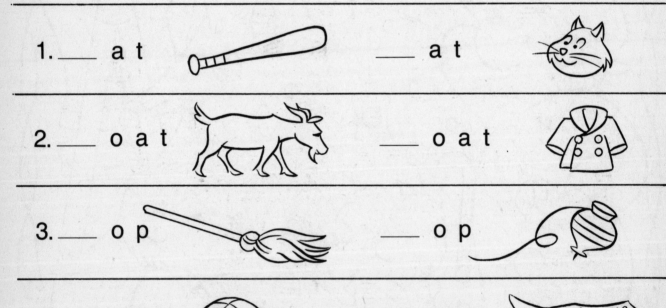

1. ___ a t   ___ a t

2. ___ o a t   ___ o a t

3. ___ o p   ___ o p

4. ___ a p   ___ a p

5. ___ u g   ___ u g

Flaky Fun

All of these snowmen seem to look exactly alike, but look again.
One is different. Can you find him?

Num-brrrs!

Sister drew a figure 8 in the ice. But where are 1, 2, 3, 4, 5, 6, and 7? Can you find them hidden in the picture?

Ballet Look-Alikes

Can you find two dancing bears who look exactly alike?

Jumping Rope

Can you find the shadow that matches Sister jumping rope?

T Time

Find at least 10 things in this picture that start with the letter **T**.

Tree Trouble

Raffish Ralph is hopping mad!
He can't find the Weasels' secret tree.
Help Ralph find the right one by circling the tree that has
exactly 7 branches.

Cookie Count

Grizzly Gran wants 10 cookies on each cookie tray. Draw more cookies, or cross out cookies, until each tray has exactly 10 cookies.

1

2

3

4

The Silly Garden

Someone's been planting silly things in Farmer Ben's garden.
Help him clean up by circling 8 things that don't belong.

Dark Park

The bears had so much fun in the park that they stayed all day. But now it's dark, and they've lost their way! Show the bears the way home.

Leapin' Leashes!

Trace the tangled leashes to find out who is walking Snuff.

Sister   Cousin Freddy   Brother

Shadow Dancing

Can you match Too-Tall to his dancing shadow?

Book Look

Actual Factual lost 10 of his books in the
Bearsonian Institution! Circle the hidden books.

Music Makers

Cross out the one thing in each row that isn't used to make music.

Match the Pairs

Sister is hanging up clothes to dry.
Help her find the socks that go together.
Draw a line to connect each matching pair.

1   2   3   4   5

A   B   C   D   E

Cake Bake

Papa, Brother, and Sister want to bake a cake for Mama's birthday. But they aren't sure what to use. Cross out the things that don't belong in a cake.

Scare Bears

Who scared Brother and Sister on Halloween night? Color each space with the number 1 in it to find out!

Halloween Hunt

Sister and Brother decorated their room for Halloween. But now they're too scared to close their eyes! Cross out 5 bats and 5 other scary things so Sister and Brother can get some sleep.

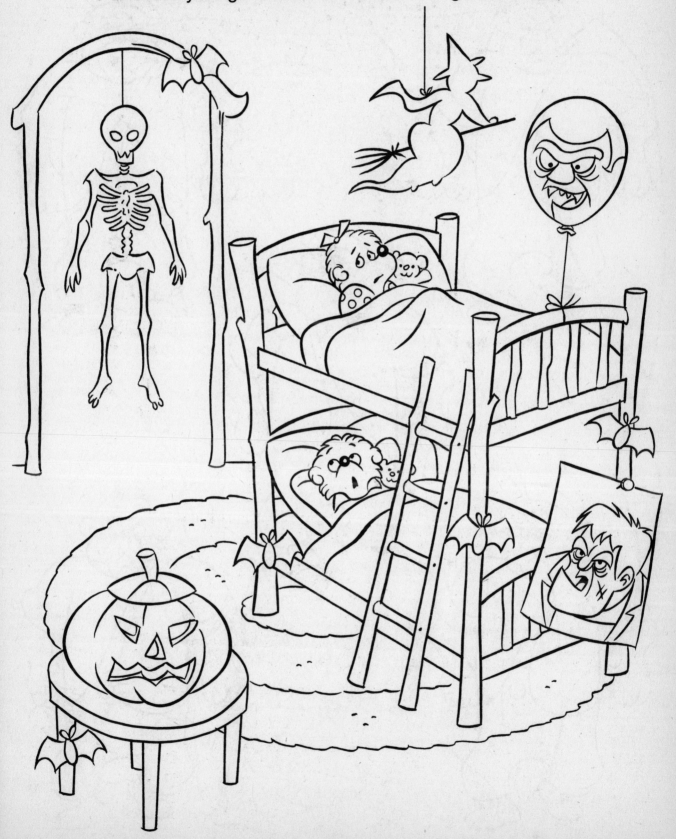

Two-Ton Twins

Can you find two pictures of Two-Ton Grizzly that look exactly alike?

Gone Fishing

Can you find the names of some of the things Papa took on his fishing trip? Look across and down. Circle the words you find.

j h a t b
p o l e o
w o r m a
m k x p t

Word List
boat
hat
hook
pole
worm

Picnic Path

Brother is late for the bears' picnic. Can you help him find the way?

Mama Match

Draw a line from each mother to her baby.

1.

A.

2.

B.

3.

C.

4.

D.

5.

E.

6.

F.

Silly Studio

While Madame Bearyshnikov's back was turned, the ballerina bears brought 9 silly things into the room. Circle the 9 things that don't belong in a ballet studio.

Whose Shoes?

Help the bear detectives solve their case.
Draw lines to connect the footprints to the
shoes that made them.

1.

A.

2.

B.

3.

C.

4.

D.

Grizzly Gran Look-Alikes

Can you find two pictures of Grizzly Gran that look exactly alike?

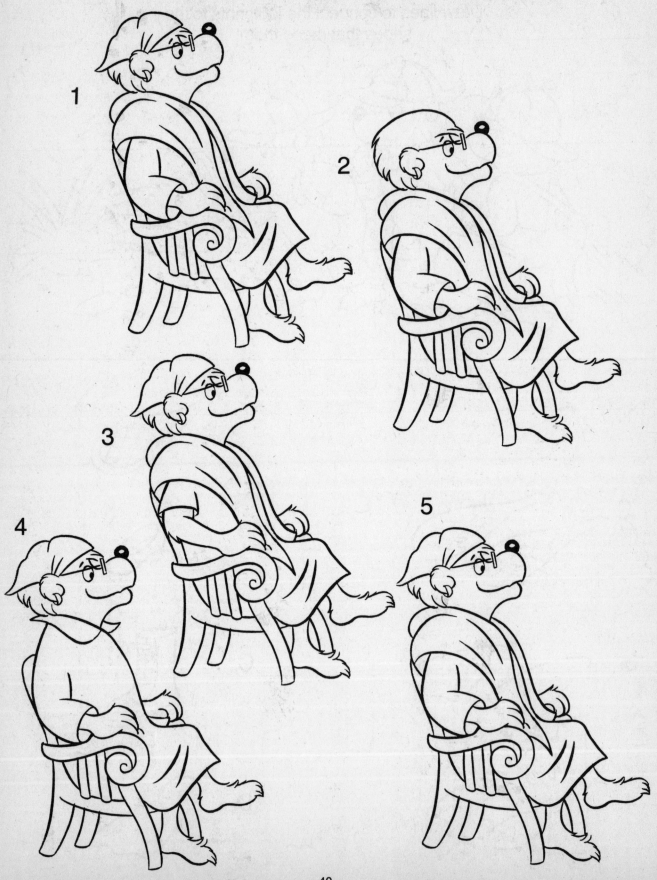

Where Is Snuff?

Mrs. Honeypot's dog can't find Snuff in the woods. Can you show her the way?

← START

41

School Days

Sister has 1 apple on her desk. Can you help
her count the apples on the chalkboard?

Circle the Circles

Mama Bear's pie is shaped like a circle. Can you find all the other things in this picture that are round like a circle?

Alphabet Art

Connect the dots from A to Z to find out what Brother painted.

Perfect Pairs

Some things go together — like Brother and Sister!
Draw lines to connect the things below that go together.

1.

A.

2.

B.

3.

C.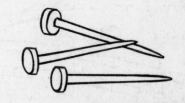

4.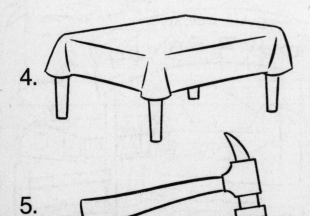

D.

5.

E.

Prancing Pony

Show Sister and her pony the way to the ranch.

High in the Sky

Sister is looking up at the sky.
What are some things she might see? Use the
picture clues to fill in the crossword below.

1–Down

2–Down

3–Down

3–Across

4–Across

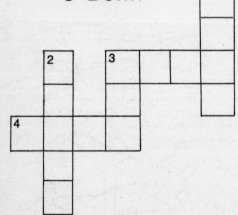

Word Bank
BIRD
CLOUD
MOON
STAR
SUN

47

Fish Fun

Brother and Sister went fishing with Grizzly Gramps.
Draw lines to connect the matching fish they caught.

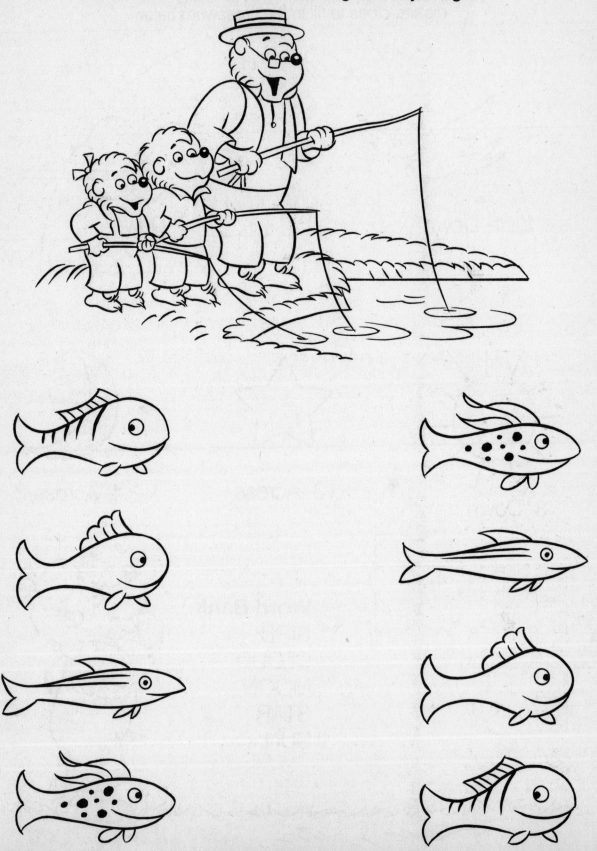

Rhyme Time

Actual Factual's names rhyme. Help the professor find
other words that rhyme. Draw lines to connect the rhyming pairs.

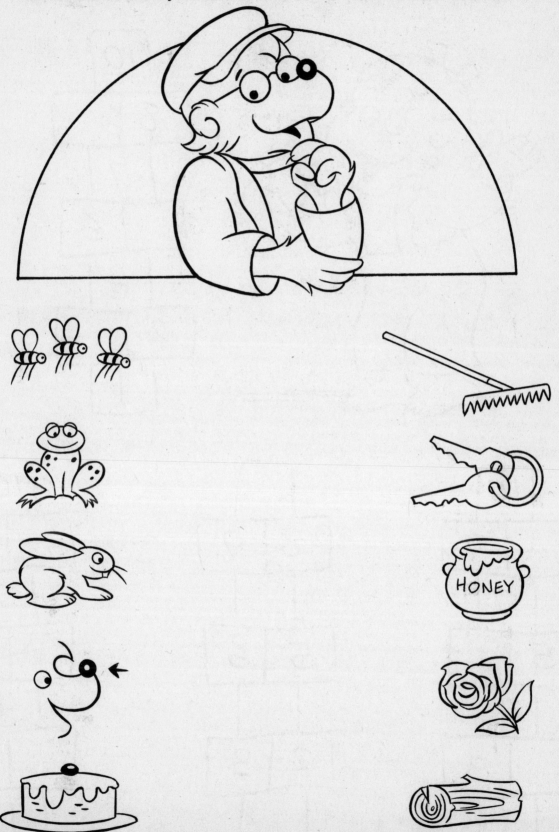

Hopscotch Helper

Sister drew hopscotch boards for all the cubs. But some of the numbers are missing. Fill in the empty boxes on each board so the bears can play.

Goofy Golf

The bears are playing miniature golf.
Can you help Brother score a hole-in-one?

Brother's Crossword

Brother and bicycle are words that begin with **B**. Use the picture clues to fill in the crossword with some other words that begin with **B**.

1–Across

1–Down

2–Across

2–Down

3–Across

Word Bank
ball
bee
bell
boat
book

Sky High

How many things can you count flying in the air?

Like Leaves

Help Scout leader Jane match each leaf she found to her chart. Draw lines to connect the matching leaves.

oak   poplar   maple   elm

B Is for Birthday

It's Brother's birthday. He's hoping for lots of presents
that start with his favorite letter — **B!**
Circle 5 presents that start with **B.**

Play Ball!

Brother wants to play baseball, but he can't find his gear! Help him by circling all the things he'll need.

Mixed-Up Fruit

Oh-oh! Brother and Sister bumped into Farmer Ben's fruit stand.
Help them by drawing a line from each piece of fruit to its basket.

Family Fun

The pictures in each row seem to look alike, but look again!
Can you find the picture that is different in each row?

Numbers Hunt

Sister can count from one to ten.
Look across and down to find the names of the
numbers in the puzzle below. Circle the words you find.

s e v e n f t
f i v e i o h
s g t t n u r
i h w e e r e
x t o n e z e

Word List
one
two
three
four
five
six
seven
eight
nine
ten

A Walk in the Woods

Can you help Cousin Freddy find Brother and Sister in the woods?

Answers

Page 2

Page 3

Page 4

Page 5

Page 6
Dress 3

Page 7

Page 8

Page 9
1. There are 4 fireflies in the jar.
2. There are 5 fireflies still free.
3. There are 9 fireflies all together.

Page 10

Page 11
7 stars

Page 12
1-C, 2-A, 3-B, 4-D

Page 13

Page 15

Page 16

1-bat/cat, 2-goat/coat, 3-mop/top, 4-cap/map, 5-bug/rug

Page 17

Snowman 4

Page 18

Page 19

3 and 5

Page 20

Shadow 5

Page 21

Page 22

Tree 5

Page 23

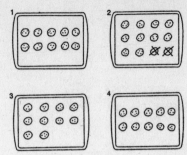

Page 24

Page 25

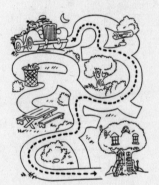

Page 26

Cousin Freddy is walking Snuff.

Page 27

Shadow 3

Page 28

Page 29

Page 30

1-C, 2-E, 3-D, 4-B, 5-A

Page 31

Page 32

A ghost

Page 33

Page 34

1 and 4

Page 35

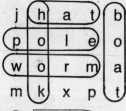

Page 36

Page 37

1-E, 2-A, 3-F, 4-C, 5-B, 6-D

Page 38

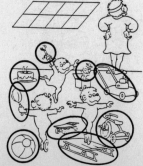

Page 39

1-B, 2-A, 3-D, 4-C

Page 40

1 and 5

Page 41

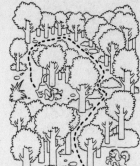

Page 42

10 apples

Page 43

Page 44

A zebra

Page 45

1-D, 2-E, 3-A, 4-B, 5-C

Page 46

Page 47

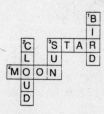

Page 48

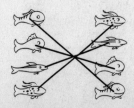

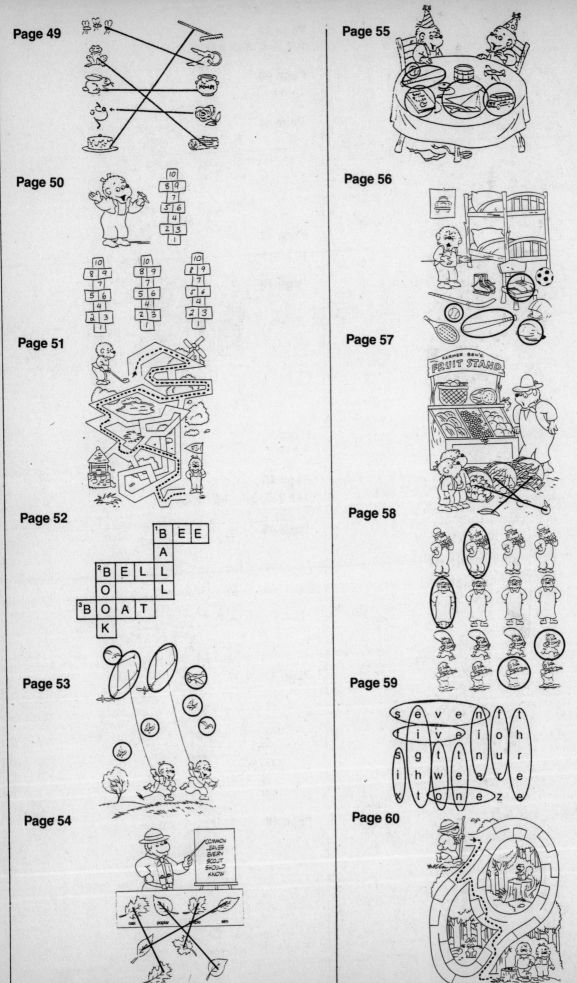

Page 49

Page 50

Page 51

Page 52

Page 53

Page 54

Page 55

Page 56

Page 57

Page 58

Page 59

Page 60